Papa's Mark

By Gwendolyn Battle-Lavert

Illustrated by Colin Bootman

VOTE! VOTE!
All MEN OF
COLOR
VOTE!

HOLIDAY HOUSE NEW YORK

Daylight crept over Lamar County. Simms and his papa were going to town. The wagon went bumpty-bump along the road. They passed large fields with grazing animals and small wooden houses that were still dark. As they rode, the fields became smaller and the houses closer together. Finally, they reached clusters of buildings decorated with voting posters and waving flags.

This was election time.

"Look!" yelled Simms. "Vote! Vote!"

"Simmer down," said Papa. "You'd wake a sleeping dog."

Simms laughed. With each bump, he bounced happily up and down in the wagon.

The men in their community met once a week to talk about the election. They met in the church and at Simms's house.

Simms always stood by his papa's side.

Papa pulled up next to the general store.
"Jump down," said Papa. "No time to waste."
Smells of apples, oranges, onions, potatoes,
and peppermint candy met Simms at the door.

"Samuel T. Blow," said Mr. Jones, the storekeeper. "You're here mighty early."

"Mornin'!" said Papa. "Our weekly shopping trip. Simms got the list."

In a clear voice, Simms read. Mr. Jones filled the box with supplies. Papa stood by, looking on.

"Well now," said Mr. Jones. "Election day in a few weeks. You colored folks must be mighty proud."

"History in the making right here in Lamar County," said Papa.

Everybody stopped. Papa was a man of few words. But when he spoke, it was important. "My papa couldn't vote. Bless his soul! But he knew if not in his time, in my time."

Simms looked up and smiled. "That's everything on the list!"

"Not yet," said Papa. "Do you want a piece of candy?"

"And take a voting poster, too," said Mr. Jones.

"Yes, sir!" said Simms.

"Thank you kindly, Mr. Jones," said Papa. He picked up the box. Simms trailed behind him.

"Samuel T.!" called Mr. Jones. "Put your mark here."

Papa turned around. Every Saturday Simms watched Papa put an *X* on the pad. Simms's gaze fell to the floor.

"Come on, Simms," said Papa, moving toward the door.

They rode home in silence.

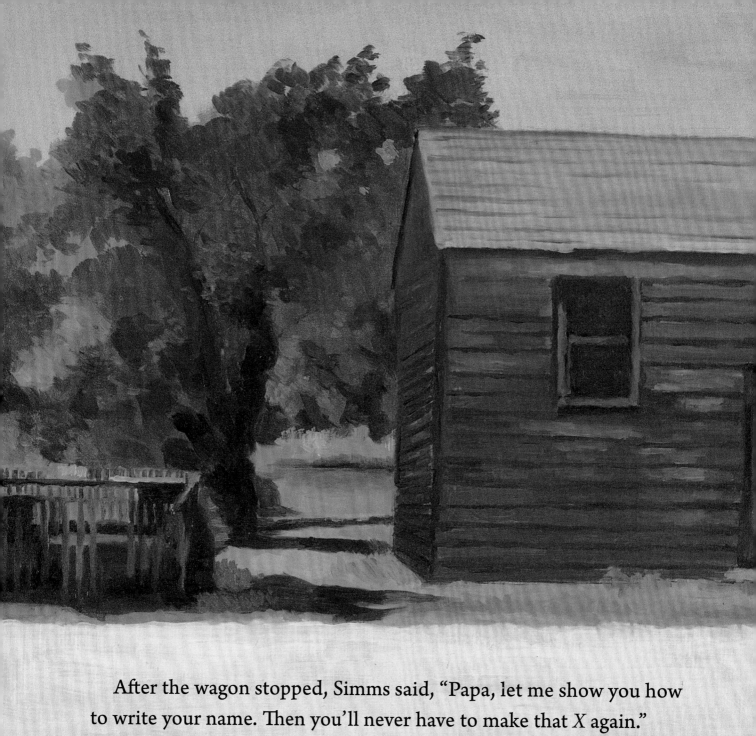

After the wagon stopped, Simms said, "Papa, let me show you how to write your name. Then you'll never have to make that *X* again."

"Simms, you got work of your own," said Papa. "Now help me carry these groceries inside."

That night, the men huddled around the kitchen table. Simms looked into scared faces. He listened.

"There's trouble brewing," one man said in a low voice. "Some folks don't want us colored voting."

"Freedom don't come easy," said Papa. "My papa taught me that."

"You go on or die," said another.

Simms stood up and waved the voting poster.

"I'm helping," said Simms. "Every house gonna get one of these."

The men laughed. The meeting went on.

Simms went to his room to make more posters.

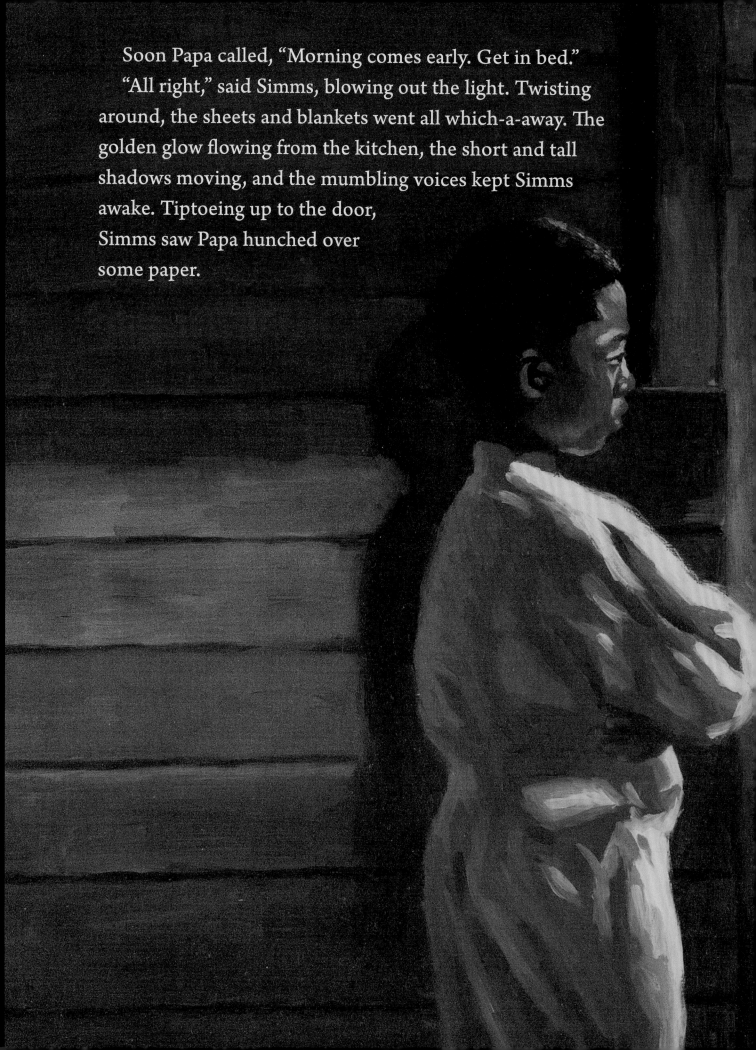

Soon Papa called, "Morning comes early. Get in bed."

"All right," said Simms, blowing out the light. Twisting around, the sheets and blankets went all which-a-away. The golden glow flowing from the kitchen, the short and tall shadows moving, and the mumbling voices kept Simms awake. Tiptoeing up to the door, Simms saw Papa hunched over some paper.

"It'll get better, Samuel," said Mama.

"This writing looks like chicken scratch," said Papa.

Mama laughed softly. "Well, mine looks like red-hot chili peppers—the letters jump all over the paper!"

"When I vote," said Papa. "I'm gonna write my name to get my ballot."

"What you doing!" said Simms, jumping into the light.

Papa looked up. Simms ran back to his room and leaped into bed.
"Papa, my eyes just keep popping open," called Simms.
Papa walked in. He pulled the homemade quilt around Simms.
Sleep came.

Before school, Simms wrote Papa's name perfectly. He left the paper on the kitchen table. That night, Simms peeked around the door as Papa worked. He saw Papa try to copy his clear, neat lines. But in the morning, Simms saw chicken scratch.

A few days later, Simms found Papa at the table.

"Simms, come over here," said Papa. "I just can't seem to write the letters like you do. Can you help?"

Simms guided his papa's hand across the paper. Papa watched every curve.

"I can read my name," said Papa. "Now I'm going to write it with your help."

Every night, Papa hunched over the table, slowly tracing the curves of his name. Every morning, Simms checked Papa's paper.

Soon Election Day was just around the corner. After school, voting posters were hammered on every house and tree. Even the animals had posters around their necks.

The night before the election, the church was full of men.

"Who's gonna go with me to vote?" asked Papa.

The men mumbled and groaned. No one agreed to come.

A tall man said, "We all got families. Who's gonna take care of them if we gone?"

"It's just one day," said Papa. "They'll be fine."

"Some folks mighty angry," another man said. "We scared what they might do."

Everyone muttered in agreement.

Papa said, "We go in peace. We go in unity."

The room was silent.

Simms said, "Papa, I'll go with you."

The men left. The meeting ended.

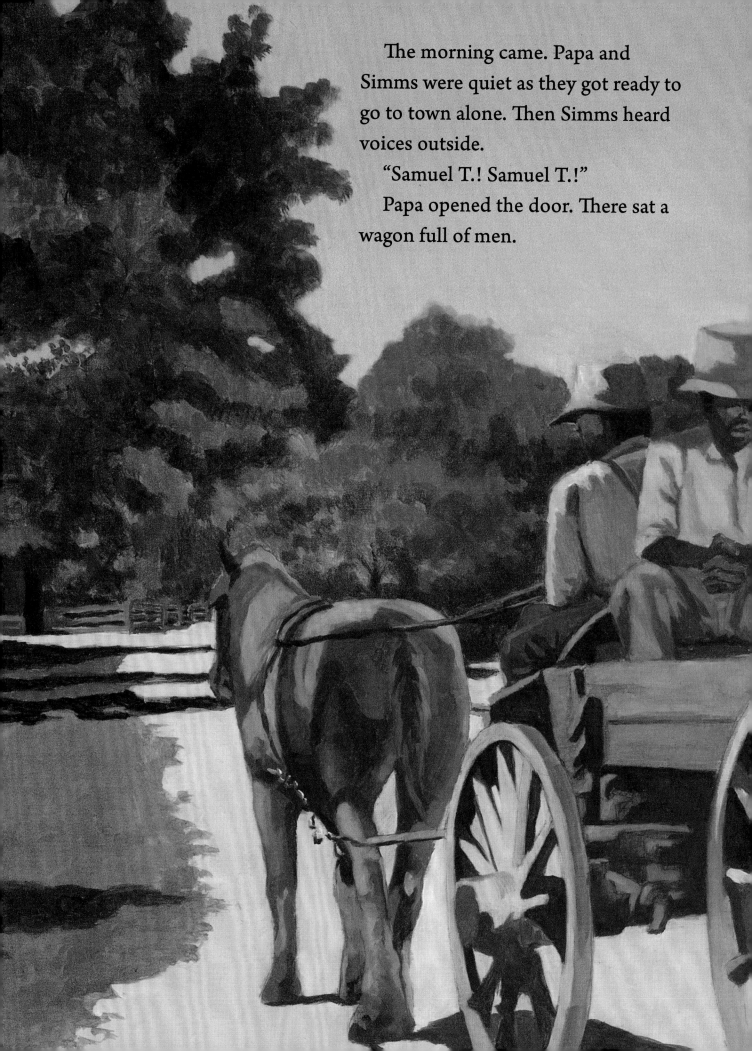

The morning came. Papa and Simms were quiet as they got ready to go to town alone. Then Simms heard voices outside.

"Samuel T.! Samuel T.!"

Papa opened the door. There sat a wagon full of men.

"Come on!" they said. "We go in unity. Simms shamed us."

The wagon took off up the road. Thumpty-thump! Bumpty-bump! Hours later, they made it to town. The wind howled like a blare of bugles. The flags flapped like snare drums. Folks crowded the street. Simms didn't recognize their hard faces. Papa got out of the wagon first.

Out of the crowd came Mr. Jones, the storekeeper. "Samuel T.,"
he said, "I'm voting with you."

The two men walked together across the town square to the
courthouse.

"I'm Samuel T. Blow," said Papa. "I've come to vote."

"Make your mark," said the clerk.

Simms said, "My papa can sign his name."

Papa wrote his name. The clerk handed him a ballot. Papa made a choice.

Then he said, "Simms, come over here. Let's put the ballot in the box together."

Simms grinned. Papa voted. Lamar County changed.

AUTHOR'S NOTE

At the end of the Civil War, the Thirteenth Amendment to the Constitution was adopted, abolishing slavery. Leaders such as Frederick Douglass insisted that freedom was not enough; the Black man must have the right to vote. Black men were finally made citizens under a provision of the Fourteenth Amendment, which became part of the Constitution in 1868.

Two years later, the Fifteenth Amendment protected the right of the Black man to vote. Although most Black Southerners could not yet read or write, they soon began to see that they could use the ballot to improve their lives. This is the period in which *Papa's Mark* is set.

Many white Southerners became angry; they wanted to recover their power. Within a few years, they found ways to do so. They required Black men to pay a poll, or voting, tax. Since most Black men were poor, they could not pay. Literacy tests were also used to keep them from voting. Many were driven from the polling places by violence. As a result, many Black Southerners could not vote. Women were given the right to vote in 1920; however, Black women found themselves under the same constraints Black men had been for so many decades.

In the 1960s, Martin Luther King Jr. and other Black leaders organized both Black and white people to demonstrate for voting rights in nonviolent ways. In 1964, the Twenty-fourth Amendment to the Constitution was adopted, barring the poll tax in elections for president, vice president, and members of Congress. That summer became known as Freedom Summer because of a massive voting rights campaign that took place in Mississippi.

In 1965, Congress passed the Voting Rights Act, which removed other obstacles that kept Black people from voting. Black people began to vote in record numbers throughout the North and the South. But issues continued.

In 2021, the John Lewis Voting Rights Advancement Act was introduced as a reform bill that would bring the Voting Rights Act of 1965 up to date, strengthening legal protections against discriminatory voting policies and practices. Americans, for the most part, believe that voting should be as easy and accessible as possible. In many cases, it is; however, in recent years, there have been more than 400 anti-voter bills that have caused unnecessary barriers for people to register to vote, vote by mail, or vote in person. This has severely compromised democracy. More importantly, the anti-voter bills do not reflect the will of the majority of the people. The late John Lewis, Georgia representative and voting rights activist, fought to bring the Voting Rights Advancement Act to fruition.

On August 24, 2021, the bill passed the House of Representatives, but it has not yet been passed into law. But John Lewis's work, which was for the equality and civil rights of all people, especially disadvantaged minority voters and marginalized communities, will not die. Americans would be compromising democracy if the people's voices were not heard and everyone could not vote.

Today, the Voting Rights Act is still as important as it was years ago, because voter suppression is still deeply linked to a troubling history of legislative laws. We must stand together. The future of our democracy depends on it. John Lewis said, "Never ever be afraid to make some noise and get in trouble, good trouble, necessary trouble."

To Janice, Carison, Jarrett, and Jonathan Adams
—G. B.-L.

To Keith Anthony Jones, "my brother"
—C.B

Text copyright © 2003, 2023 by Gwendolyn Battle-Lavert • Illustrations copyright © 2003 by Colin Bootman • All Rights Reserved
HOLIDAY HOUSE is registered in the U.S. Patent and Trademark Office. • Printed and bound in September 2022 at C&C Offset, Shenzhen, China.
The artwork was created with oil paint on canvas. • www.holidayhouse.com
Second Edition

1 3 5 7 9 10 8 6 4 2

Library of Congress has cataloged the prior edition as follows:

Battle-Lavert, Gwendolyn. | Papa's mark / by Gwendolyn Battle-Lavert; illustrated by Colin Bootman.—1ˢᵗ ed.
p. cm.
Summary: After his son helps him learn to write his name, Samuel T. Blow goes to the courthouse in his
Southern town to cast his ballot on the first election day ever on which African Americans were allowed to vote.
ISBN: 0-8234-1650-X (hardcover)
1. African Americans—History—1863-1877—Juvenile fiction. 2. Southern States—History—1865-1877—Juvenile fiction.
[1. African Americans—History—1863-1877—Fiction. 2. Southern States—History—1865-1877—Fiction.
3.Voting—Fiction. 4.Literary—Fiction. 5.Fathers and sons—Fiction.] I. Bootman, Colin, ill. II. Title.
PZ7.B32446 Pap 2022   [E]—dc21   2001024486
ISBN: 978-0-8234-5370-2 (hardcover)